إن شاء الله

INSHALLAH

ISBN: 9798495198661

Prophet Muhammad (PBUH) stated in his farewell sermon,
'O people, An Arab has no superiority over non-Arab, nor a non-Arab has any superiority over Arab, also white has no superiority over black nor does black have any superiority over white, except by piety and righteousness. All humans are from Adam and Adam is from dust.'

'Above all, love each other deeply because love covers over a multitude of sins.'

\- 1 Peter 4:8

'Let us not love with words or speech but with actions and in truth.'
-1 John 3:18

Allah will say on the Day of Resurrection: *'Where are those who love one another for My glory's sake. Today I will shelter them in My shade, today there is no shade but only My shade.'*

CONTENTS

CHAPTER ONE

'Mummy, come!'

'What is it, Yaz? I'm making your breakfast.'

Yasmin, or Yaz as I call her, is my 6-year-old daughter.

'Mummy come, the telly is all funny and I can't find my programme.'

I sighed and said, 'Seriously, I put it on for you five minutes ago.'

Yaz is shouting louder, 'Mummy, mummy, there is a strange man on the telly with a black mask. He is on all the CBeebies and I don't want to watch him. I want to watch Tracy Beaker again.'

Really, I know she can exaggerate things sometimes to get me to solve her problems. 'I'm coming, give me two minutes,' I call out to her. I walk into the lounge to see Yaz standing in front of the television blocking the screen. 'What is it?' I ask.

'Look Mummy!' she exclaims, as she steps aside pointing the remote control towards the television, flicking away.

She's right, every time she presses a button nothing happens. That's strange. I take the remote control from her and hit it on my hand, maybe the batteries are dead. I play around with the volume and turn it off and on for a few times, but everything seems to be working, except that I can't get the image of the masked man off the screen.

As I stare at the Arabic writing in the background, I wonder if there's a glitch in the system and the *Caliphate* series that I have been watching on Netflix is streaming across all channels. I stand transfixed watching the men standing around with guns and their faces covered up.

Suddenly, they move aside and push a small boy to the front of the camera. I recognise that child, it's the Prime Minister's son. He must be around nine or ten years old. It dawns on me that this isn't a movie, so I hurry Yaz out of the room without frightening her.

'Yaz, why don't you go and get dressed and I'll try to fix the telly?'

I am pushing her out of the room, and I tell her that I'll be with her in five minutes. I don't want her coming back to find me. Max, the Prime Minister's son, holds up a newspaper with yesterday's date and starts talking, but his words are barely a whisper as tears roll down his face.

He has one of those orange suits on which I have seen before on other people who were captured by ISIS. He looks so small and pale; all the blood has drained from his face. I have never in my life seen a child with such fear in his eyes, actually I have never seen any human with such fear. It dawns on me that this is a real-life scenario and it is definitely not a movie. My throat tightens as I try to blink away my tears.

I feel an uncomfortable sensation in my stomach. That feeling when your cheeks start to get a strange pulling sensation just before you throw up. He is whispering something, but I can't hear what he is saying, so I walk closer to the telly and turn it up at the same time.

One of the men steps forward and puts his hand on Max's shoulder firmly and tells him to read the paper that they have given him. He says, 'I'm Max Bernard and I have been kidnapped by ISIS' and then he adds, 'Daddy please do what they want, I'm scared and I want to come home.'

Tears streaming down his face, he starts sobbing uncontrollably. His body is shaking with fear. It looks like he is struggling to even sit up straight. He looks up at the man and it seems as if he is looking at him for some sort of acknowledgement.

Just then one of the other men steps forward and says, 'We want our brothers released. You have the names of our brothers, we want them back here with us and if you don't arrange their release within 24 hours, Max will have to pay for their freedom. We will not be disobeyed and ignored any longer. We will be declaring victory over the world soon.' Then all the men start shouting "Allahu Akbar, Allahu Akbar, Allahu Akbar" while waving fists in the air.

CHAPTER TWO

After 9/11 British intelligence agencies captured a lot of ISIS terrorists at the highest level and they are all anticipating a trial sometime soon. The reality is that when it comes to terrorist trials, they can't just happen overnight and tend to drag on for years.

Sometimes, when I read the news online and read that so and so is still waiting for his trial after three years in prison, I can't believe how quickly time has gone by. Well for me it has, but I doubt it has for them, especially in America where they can hold on to someone charged with terrorism for years before they go to trial.

My mind wanders for a minute and I see the man in the front lifts his arm signalling the other men to be quiet and then he says, 'Inshallah you will be granting our brothers' freedom tonight. We are giving you until tomorrow morning, otherwise Max will pay the price, Allahu Akbar.'

The television goes black for a few seconds and then back to the BBC and, a very bewildered, Huw Edwards starts talking. He looks just as confused as, what I suppose, the rest of the nation is. He explains that the BBC was infiltrated, and they managed to bypass all security and override the programmes with their broadcast.

He very quickly adds that the BBC has state-of-the-art security and infiltrating it is highly impossible. Well, I can imagine that if there is ever a security breach, it can cost the BBC millions of viewers and they can't afford any lawsuits as it will damage their reputation, never mind financially cripple them. We all know how they hound people down who don't pay their TV license and even put old people in prison, so they can't be that financially secure.

'We will be going live to Downing Street shortly as we have just had a call from the Prime Minister's office and he wants to make a brief statement,' Huw informs us.

A picture of London is on the screen with the big wheel and Buckingham Palace. On a grey day outside the picture reminds us of a sunny London and not the real London as of today. A few minutes later the image changes to the front door at Downing Street. There is a podium set up outside the door and a microphone.

The door opens and out comes Prime Minister Charles Bernard followed by his wife and his deputy. The Prime Minister looks terrible; Helen Bernard looks like she has aged ten years overnight. The Prime Minister's skin looks like glass; you can see he hasn't slept for many nights. Mrs Bernard's agony is visible and any mother can understand her pain.

He stands for a minute with his head bowed down to compose himself, then lifts his head up and says, 'A week ago Max was kidnapped and we were advised by the British Intelligence that in order to protect him and his security it was absolutely imperative to keep it quiet as we don't want to risk endangering Max's life any further. All the different departments are working together around the clock to try and find Max. We have called in on our Middle Eastern allies to help track him and we are grateful for the assistance in trying to find him.'

He sounds a bit like a well-rehearsed actor. He stops talking and takes a few deep breaths. You can see his shoulders start to shake a little and his voice becomes very small. He stops to compose himself and someone moves forward with a bottle of water. He takes a few sips and continues. 'As you can understand, I am not at liberty to give any more information. All I can say is that this country does not want to be held to ransom and let evil dictate to us.' .

As he says this, his wife lets out a whimper and starts to shake. He turns to her and quickly adds, 'I will keep you updated if we receive any more news. I ask that you please keep Max and our family in your thoughts and prayers, thank you.'

He takes her hand and they both, with the Deputy Prime Minister, walk back into Number 10. A very brief statement, not giving a lot away. I suppose he can't say much for security reasons. Although he has made it clear that even though it is his son's life at stake, he will not be persuaded to release the terrorists. They are probably so close to rescuing Max that they know they won't need to release any prisoners or who knows, maybe by the time the deadline comes he might release a couple to secure Max's release. Nobody knows, we always just find out once it's over.

****

Wow! A week has passed since he was taken. I cannot even imagine what hell it must be for them. So-poor Max has already been living this nightmare for a week while we have been going about with our normal routines. I think about the British Intelligence out in the desert somewhere in camouflage tents, tanks roaming about dust-filled villages looking for Max. Men with night vision goggles and large AK47's going from house to house working around the clock to try to locate him. For a few minutes, it seems like a movie.

'Mummy, where's my pancakes that you promised? I'm hungry and I want juice, please. Can I have Nutella and fruit on my pancakes and honey?' Yaz asks. 'Mummy, are you listening to me?' she says again as she turns my face towards herself so that she can look at me in the eyes. She always does this when she talks to me. She likes eye contact and 100% attention.

Yaz isn't concerned with a kidnapping or prisoner swap. For a split second, I feel a little irritable as I want to continue watching the television just in case something else pops up. Then I feel her little hands cupping my face and my love for her is overwhelming. I smile and lean in and kiss her nose.

I don't think anyone can make pancakes faster than me while watching the news on their phone. The rest of the day seems to go by in a blur. The television stations continue reporting about Max's disappearance. A lot of the television stations have cancelled their normal programmes and have put up footage about Max and the terrorists. Surprisingly, many experts who were interviewed from their homes explained that a prisoner swap isn't always possible.

Middle Eastern countries are more likely to make a swap between themselves as negotiating amongst themselves is so much easier than dealing with countries like the UK and America's bureaucracy. Those that are mostly kidnapped are missionaries, doctors or people transporting supplies or part of a convoy. Some television stations are trying to vary the programmes, still keeping up with the ISIS theme in a way and are talking about how many people have become disillusioned with living the life as a fighter or the wife of a fighter. When interviewed they say they never realised they would be living in slums, with rationed food supplies and having their lives controlled 24/7.

CHAPTER THREE

Living in Raqqa, Syria, they had to give up on the free life they led in other countries. Gone are the days of having access to mobile phones, the internet, Netflix etc. Life is extremely restricted and regimented. Everyone is very suspicious of each other and people are living in fear in case their neighbours inform the leaders of ISIS that they have done something wrong when they haven't actually done anything. People who travelled to fight this good cause and live the dream of becoming holy in a way, are now trying to escape and reunite with their families in the UK or other countries. However, they know they'll be arrested if they try to return, so they are getting their families to plead innocence on their behalf.

It appears that the appeal system is working as quite a number of people have returned to the UK and aren't arrested or they are slipping through at the ports where they aren't marked as suspicious. Some are smuggled through on the back of trucks; their families are paying a lot of money to smuggle them back into the UK. There will be repercussions for these people as the newspapers will now be hounding them down and vigilantes will be out looking for revenge. All of a sudden it will be an eye for an eye and all that malarkey. People who have never even set foot in a church suddenly start quoting the Bible. Some channels have footage of refugee camps in places like Syria and even Calais, France showing the people who escaped from ISIS and how difficult their lives were in Raqqa.

It is surprising how they have managed to find this stuff now, or have they shown it before and I have never been interested? I do however remember reading the newspaper about a convoy going over to take medical supplies and food to one of the refugee camps in Syria and one of the volunteers was captured and beheaded by ISIS. Here was an ordinary man trying to show compassion and do some good in the world and he was killed for it. So heart-breaking for the families, it will make anyone lose trust in humanity. It seems about 900 people from the UK have travelled to Syria to join the conflict, I would think there is a lot more as I am sure not everyone is recorded.

The television crew have managed to find a couple of English schoolgirls who ran away to marry terrorists. Apparently, their husbands were killed. One of the young girls says she has been married three times already and lost all her husbands to martyrdom. Three husbands! Wow, heart-breaking, to think you are killing yourself to go to heaven and the Quran specifically says you will not see paradise if you kill anyone and then the heartache that a family goes through losing loved ones. I'm not sure how I would feel about being married three times knowing each time as soon as you fall in love with someone they go off and kill themselves. Does the pain lessen after a while or don't they really fall in love and they just go through the emotions of being a dutiful wife?

Some of these girls are waiting to hear if they will be stripped of their citizenship. They have heard of other women losing their citizenship because they have dual nationalities, or their husbands who are part of ISIS, are from other European countries. The UK acknowledges that they are married now and should be living with their husbands, although it seems most of their husbands are either in prison or dead. So, they are in no man's land as nobody wants to accept responsibility for them. It is an expense no government really wants as they will have to look after them for the rest of their lives since no one will want to employ them.

We all know that the courts will rule in their favour eventually and they will be allowed to travel back home to fight their cases. They'll be a burden on the state and financially, it will cost a lot. They will be given accommodation away from their families to protect them and paid an income to survive as they aren't able to work and if the countries decide to prosecute the cases, it can drag on for years.

Of course, not many women want to be interviewed as they are scared the other women in the camp will attack them or their children will be bullied. Religious women are very dutiful and feel it's important to know their place and don't want to be seen as some sort of celebrity. The two girls interviewed are both hoping the UK will show clemency and allow them back in.

I have no sympathy for the English girls. They ran away and knew that their husbands-to-be, would be killing innocent people and now they want us to take them back without asking questions. They want to be allowed back to continue their lives and the taxpayers must look after them. Why should they be allowed back? I hear they are British and have rights. Really, *surely*, they gave up these rights when they married terrorists.

So, while they were playing housewives and looking after their husbands, they weren't worried about being British. Now their husbands are dead, they have to fend for themselves and all of a sudden, they remember their rights as British citizens. The BBC Breakfast interviews a girl from Barbados. She is apparently the only woman from Barbados, together with her husband, who joined ISIS. She has become some sort of a celebrity back home, but not in a good way. She stresses that she never wanted to be known as the only woman from Barbados to join ISIS and then flee to a refugee camp when the going got tough.

She is covered from head to toe in black with a very Barbadian accent. It sounds like they have dubbed her voice, it just doesn't sound right. They grew up drinking, going to parties and then her husband met a man who introduced him to a few other men from the local mosque. She said slowly her husband got more and more interested in Islam. He started going to the mosque regularly and then she started hanging out with other wives. Gradually things started to change for them. Life got better, their married life improved, they joined the community. She loved it, she really felt at peace. They both had their Shahadas, they started praying five times a day, stopped drinking, eating pork etc. She started to wear a hijab. They evaluated their lives and decided to convert to Islam.

She said they lived like this this for a couple of years and then her husband decided they needed to move to Raqqa and join the fight. He gradually became obsessed with wanting to fight the good cause, so to speak. She was nervous and they discussed it with the other families who warned them not to do it. She said it was as if her husband couldn't hear what the others were saying. He had become brainwashed. She said there was never any question of her staying behind because, as a dutiful wife, she followed her husband. She hoped once they got there he would realise his mistake and they would return home. She packed up everything and put it in storage as she was convinced they would be home soon. He was killed within a year of moving there and she now has to raise her son on her own. She decided to leave Syria as she doesn't want to have to bury her son as well. She felt if they had stayed he would have followed in his father's footsteps, so she wanted to distance herself from ISIS. She needs help from her family and mosque to raise her son. She said she saw heads in bins, so-called traitors, and nobody flinched or said anything. ISIS beheaded their own if they thought they were traitors.

CHAPTER FOUR

The news is dominated by the nightmare of Max's kidnapping and Facebook has come alive with Max as the main topic of conversation. Everyone seems to have an opinion and only one subject matter on their minds. Photos of Max are most people's profile photos with the words *"Pray for Max"* written across it. My church has put up a message encouraging us all to pray and if we need to talk to anyone we just call.

I walk to our local One-Stop to buy a few random bits. People are just talking to anyone who will listen. They just want to be able to discuss it with anyone. I'm standing in the queue and I can't stop thinking about how they have managed to recruit such intelligent people to work for them and we are left with a bunch of halfwits that can't manage to work a till. Seriously, who knows how to hack into the BBC and take over the main stations, bypass that unbelievable security and broadcast from what seems like the middle of nowhere? It just doesn't seem real. They should rather use that amount of intelligence to do good in the world.

When you work for an organisation like that, surely you must be able to see what kind of people they are. Are these people brainwashed? It's the only explanation I can think of. Who thinks suicide bombings and beheading people is justified in the name of religion? I remember when I converted from being Jewish to a Christian my ex-mother-in-law was convinced I had been brainwashed and joined a cult. She was agnostic and just couldn't get her head around me becoming a Christian. She was scared I was going to make my ex-husband sell our house and give all our money to the church. She hired someone to talk to me as she could not understand how someone who has their own mind would want to join a cult as she called it and follow the Bible. I remember her asking to meet with me on a Sunday and I said was going to church and that was the final nail, so to speak, for her. She screamed at my ex and said he needs to do something as I'll brainwash Yasmin and will destroy her life.

She said that we will end up living in a community and I'll change my daughter's personality and she won't be able to think for herself. I think she thought I was going to convince my then-husband to move to Utah and join the Mormons or even the Amish given the way she carried on. She then took matters into her own hands and emailed all my friends telling them to be careful of me as I would probably try and recruit them for my cult, as if I had the power and, all of a sudden, it was *my* cult. Many avoided me and gradually I lost a lot of friends. It was only years later that I found out she had done this.

I get to the front of the queue and listen to an old man next to me talking about dropping a bomb on them. He said that will sort them out. Someone asked, 'What about the children?' He waves his arm in the air and says, 'Nonsense, they are future terrorists.' I decide it's time to get out of the shop.

I remember when I lived in Boston, Massachusetts and made friends with a Mormon family who lived with us on campus. My ex-husband and I lived on campus at Harvard, he studied and worked there and I was fortunate enough to also study South American Tribes and Rituals. Harvard is a prestigious university and you have to be extremely intelligent to study there. The entrance exams are by no means a walk in the park. As you can imagine, in class you are in competition with the best of the best and you are vying to be one of the top students.

Anyway, my mind is running wild and I remember Justin was at Harvard Law and a very devoted Mormon. He and his wife, Christy, had four children and weren't planning on stopping at four. His wife was unbelievable, the perfect wife, mother and friend. So sweet and caring and glowed as a Christian. At Harvard, you have professors who are Mormons and I somehow struggled with this idea – how can super-intelligent people believe an ordinary man who claimed to have had many visions from God telling him he would start the true Christian Church? What is the true Christian Church since there are so many denominations?

I'm sorry if I'm sceptical. I know God uses ordinary people all the time, the prophets were ordinary people, but they absolutely loved and, at the same time, feared God in a wonderful way. To me, it doesn't make sense why God would give Joseph Smith the golden plates that deviate from his original word: the Bible. I just can't understand why such intellectual people join groups like this and can't see the truth. Have they been brainwashed too? I know I get the same reaction when people find out I'm a

Christian and actually go to church. They think like my ex-mother-in-law and think I belong to some cult.

I get home and turn the television straight back on. I cannot even imagine the hell that poor boy must be living in at this very moment. I just imagine him sitting in a room not knowing what's happening to him, eating foods he doesn't know and hearing a language he doesn't understand. One minute he is at his best friend's party and the next he is in a room in a foreign country. He must be so confused, the friend who he trusted, and his parents too, how could they have done this to him. I cannot imagine living in such fear. Fear is a powerful emotion that can destroy you as a person. He has been living in a week of hell. Just like him, his parents are also going through a week of pain and fear. Knowing their child's life is in their hands. There have been requests for prisoner swaps before and most of the time they have been denied. If a prisoner swap is granted, countries will think of the UK as a soft touch and try and get all their prisoners released by kidnapping a high-profiled personality. They don't even try negotiating with America as there is more chance of hell freezing over than a prisoner swap. How can the Prime Minister now justify making a prisoner swap? He can't change the rules because of his son, or can he?

I know as a parent, I will do whatever it takes to make sure my child is safe. I will give anyone anything to make sure Yaz gets home safely. Even if it means freeing the world's worst terrorists. Then again, I'm not the prime minister and don't have the weight of the country on my shoulders and, anyway, he isn't allowed to make decisions on his own. He has a team of advisors who will tell him if it's a "yes" or "no" even if we think that it is ultimately his decision. Donald Trump is of course a completely different kettle of fish; that man goes rouge all the time. His advisors can't contain him and if they try, he fires them. Will he make a second term or will he be the first President of the United States I have ever known to be voted out after one term?

I can't stop thinking about poor Max sitting in some room with a mattress on the floor as you see in the movies. The more I think about it the more my heart aches for him. There is no one to hold him, no one to tell him everything will be alright. I wonder if he knows what will happen to him if there isn't a prisoner swap. We must remember the prisoners they want to be released aren't a few guys who ripped off a chippy or shoplifted from your local Tesco's. These are men who have orchestrated the deadliest suicide bombings in the world. They have killed and maimed thousands of people. They can't be let loose to be able to carry on causing unthinkable atrocities. How do these men look after a child for a week, feed him and know they will most likely be killing him? Most of these men are family men with children at home. Do they have no attachment to mankind that they can so easily kill someone?

I decide that I need a breath of fresh air so Yaz and I go out for a walk. She grabs her bag with a few toys as she likes to take her friends, as she calls them, along for the walk. We bump into Vakkas from the fish and chips shop. He is Kurdish and says it is the worst day for him as people say it's his kind of people doing the killing. They say, 'Turkish people are terrorists.' He was born in Turkey but constantly reminds me he is Kurdish.

Accusing him of something that has nothing to do with him is the mentality of people who aren't open minded and, in my opinion, very hard to explain the reality to. People always need someone to put the blame on. Ironically it doesn't stop them from buying kebabs and fish and chips from him and at the same time calling him a terrorist. They stand arguing with him and blaming his people for this mess. He says he can't say anything as he is scared and doesn't want to add fuel to the fire. I really feel for him, being foreign myself. We stand out like sore thumbs in a small village. They think they are so diverse with a few black people and a few foreigners like us. We have to stick together as we will never be accepted and be part of Stonesfield, Oxfordshire. Most people have grown up in the village, marry each other and even, usually after university, return home to live back in the village. There are families of third generations living Stonesfield.

Vakkas said to me, 'I have lived in this village for over 12 years, I have my wife and children here and these people are blaming me for the kidnapping of the prime minister's son. What will happen to my wife if they start accusing her? Her English is so bad. She is from my village. I'm scared they'll attack her. She wears a hijab, and people always think of women who wear headscarves as terrorists.' Vakkas stops and then adds, 'What do they think that she is hiding under her hijab, a bomb?' He mumbles 'They're idiots.' We both know they are probably bigots.

I tell him, 'Make sure she stays at home as much as possible or take her to your brother's house so she can be safe. Best make sure she always has you or your brother with her as you know these people, you know their small minds.' I remind him of the time when he shouted at a woman because she wasn't looking after her child. She was too busy on her phone in the shop and her child ran out into the road in front of a car. Vakkas ran out from behind the counter to the road and grabbed the child. He saved her child's life and then, because he was so upset that someone could be so blasé about their child's life, he started screaming at her and told her to pay more attention to her child. She then started having a go at him and called the police. The worst is the police actually turned up, of course they didn't do much, just spoke to both of them and drove off. So, a robbery they don't turn up for but a bigot of a woman who calls the police because the guy who saved her child's life shouted at her... So glad the police have their priorities right. He shakes his head. It's now because of these kinds of parents, he started to keep lollipops at the counter to give to the children so he can keep them occupied while their parents are on their phones.

I say, 'Let's face it, these idiots will always want a kebab or fish and chips, and they know nobody else will put up with their nonsense or even work the long hours. He shakes his head again and walks back into his shop. I really feel sorry for him.

Why they feel the need to blame him is beyond me. You can't trust these chavs; next, they'll throw a brick through his window.

Yaz and I arrive at the local park. We spot some of the other children from school. I sit under a tree while she plays with them. I love the way she keeps on running back to have little chats and inform me about the activities on the playground. I tell her we will pop into the local pub and buy some juice and snacks and she can use the toilet. It is packed when we get inside. Seems like everyone wants to meet up and talk about Max.

We make our way to the bar and order drinks in bottles and packets of crisps and nuts. I notice quite a few parents from her school. I don't feel like chatting with other people so I just wave, take our things and make our way out. It is quite chilly today but it is better than sitting inside a crowded pub. Kids don't feel the cold. Yaz is running around with her friends from school, screaming and laughing. I love seeing them have so much fun.

Once we get back home, I immediately turn the telly on and I'm constantly flicking through the TV channels. It is the same thing regurgitated over and over again, yet no update from Downing Street. I make dinner and the evening passes by in a haze. You would have thought it was my family that the incident happened to with the way I am worrying. It is times like this that you can see a country come together. I look at Yaz and it really breaks my heart to think about Max and here my beautiful daughter is sitting without a care in the world. Eating her favourite food, all snuggled up with a blanket, watching a movie with the cat on the little DVD player I bought her. She has her earphones plugged-in and every few minutes she is laughing at something. To see the pleasure on her face makes me so happy. I can't help it, but give her a kiss on her head and say "I love you to the moon and back". It's our little thing. She says "I love you" and I say "I love you to the moon and back".

CHAPTER FIVE

There is still no news of how the kidnapping took place. Is he still in the country or were they able to smuggle him out? Where would they have smuggled him to? I prayed, 'Please Father God, don't let him be in Turkey, you know poor Vakkas will get blamed and attacked. Please, Father, protect him and his family.' I'm thinking maybe they have taken him to Iran or Iraq. Then again, they could have taken him to Raqqa, the home of ISIS. Where else would they take him? There, no questions will be asked. I start praying for poor Max again. I have a long bath and just can't bring myself to go to bed. I cover myself with the blanket on the sofa, watching some reruns of *Bake Off* and eventually fall asleep.

I wake up and my phone says it is 3:07am. I check in on Yaz to make sure she is ok. She has kicked off her duvet. I cover her up. Soon it will be dawn and it will get cold again. I'm wide awake now. I put the telly back on and sit watching episode after episode of *Grey's Anatomy*. This is the second time I'm watching this series, but it is an easy watch and I can forward sections that annoy me. Yaz comes into the lounge for a morning cuddle. We go into the kitchen and start making breakfast. I have the volume of the TV turned up so I can hear if anything happens. Yaz wants toast with peanut butter and raspberry jam. I make a few slices, cut up some fruit and make tea. We head back into the lounge and have a little breakfast picnic. The telly is on BBC 1, I realise if any channel is going to be taken over again by ISIS it is going to be a BBC channel.

We aren't sure if we are going to church this morning as I don't want to miss out on any news, then again it will be important as we need to come together and pray for Max and the family. We need to pray for the nation as well and that those narrow-minded bigots don't start attacking innocent people.

At 9am precisely the doors to Downing Street open and the Prime Minister comes out. He looks like he is struggling to breathe; it is absolutely heart-breaking watching him. He stands for a couple of seconds which feel like minutes and then says, 'I just want to thank you all for your prayers and knowing that you are standing by my wife and me is a comfort that is beyond words. I cannot express the pain we are going through as a family. Thinking of the pain our beloved Max, who is the kindest, most loving and caring boy and who we terribly miss, is going through is beyond comprehension. We are making extremely difficult decisions and ask that you please carry on praying. We will keep you updated. Thank you.'

There are few voices shouting out in the background, 'Prime Minster can you answer a few questions?'

The deputy jumps in and says, 'No questions at this time, thank you.'

They all go back into the house and the door shuts very quickly. The television cameras continue filming for a little while longer and then the BBC correspondent starts talking. I'm not really a fan of this man but he actually seems quite sincere today. I pressed the mute button as Yaz is talking and I don't want her asking too many questions. I tell her to go and brush her teeth, get dressed and make her bed. I take the dishes into the kitchen and have my phone beside me just in case something happens.

We go to church and I'm glad we have gone as everyone is there. It's packed and Cliff, the vicar, says that he felt today's sermon isn't appropriate and that it will be Spirit lead. The worship team play a few more than usual worship songs and they bring in bean bags for those who want to just sit and pray. People start huddling together to form prayer groups. The children go off to class as usual. Once church ends, we all stand around talking, drinking tea and eating cake. One thing Christians love is fellowship, but somehow it just doesn't seem right. I wonder if fellowship is something Christians prefer to the actual religion.

Back home, Yaz and I camp out in the lounge with a carpet picnic. We buy a rotisserie chicken, baguette, snacks, juice and fruit at Morrisons. We are feasting away, and I only run to the loo and straight back, not wanting to miss out on any updates. It seems like nothing happened while we were at church. We are watching *13 going on 30*. Yaz loves this movie and I can watch it without worrying that my mind is wandering all the time. I keep checking my phone to see if the BBC has any updates. A notifications pops up on my phone to say my phone activity has risen by 22%; I'm surprised it isn't higher.

'Yaz, Mummy might just have to watch the news quickly as I am waiting to watch something very important. We might have to stop the movie for five minutes. Is that okay?' I am pre-empting her.

Yaz and I have not stopped eating, we nibble all afternoon while sitting on the sofa; I think it's my nerves. Usually if I am nervous, I can't eat; today I'm like an eating machine. That's what we, my brother and I, used to call my sister, as we fed her our sweets as small children. We were scared she would die if we stopped feeding her. Probably it would have been better if we had not fed her, she has always struggled with her weight and been overweight her whole life.

I change the channel to the BBC. There, before us, are six men dressed in very dark camouflage with their faces covered by black balaclavas. My heart skips a beat.

'Yaz, babe, why don't you go and play in your room for a few minutes as mummy wants to watch this news, it's very boring and it is for grownups. Go and play with your karaoke machine a little bit and then we can have a contest later.' I say this without sounding panicky and at the same time ushering her out of the door.

I missed the first couple of minutes as I was trying to get Yaz out of the room. I see this small pale little boy. Max's complexion has changed completely, he looks different somehow, aged. It's what fear can do to you. I remember once hearing a story about a woman who was sitting one night brushing her hair and as she looked up she saw a man standing behind her. He had apparently escaped from a mental asylum close by. Every time she tried to stop brushing her hair, he would get extremely agitated. He was mesmerised by the way she brushed it and the downward strokes of the hairbrush. She brushed her hair all night long. Tale goes that by morning she was completely grey. I doubt this is true.

CHAPTER SIX

Max is dressed in a very bright orange jumpsuit. Five of the men have large guns and the one in the middle has a large knife. They start talking in Arabic and stop after a few minutes. I think they must be in Syria; the building looks so dilapidated. It is all concrete and there is a very old wooden desk with cheap kitchen chairs. It actually looks like there are bullet holes in the walls. Max is sitting on one of the chairs, he looks so small. He is crying and at the same time starts reading from a card. It is difficult to make out what he is saying. One of the men steps forward and says, 'My name is Majid Elsheikh and I am a leader of ISIS. You tried to cripple ISIS but today we will cripple you, Mr Prime Minister, Allahu Akbar, Allahu Akbar, Allahu Akbar.' He points his gun at Max and Max lets out a cry, he sounds like a wounded animal. I hear a cry escape from my mouth at the same time.

'I, Max Bernard, must pay the price for my country's incompetence,' he says with a quivering voice. It appears they have decided there will be no prisoner swap. Max says, 'ISIS has been very patient. These are not new negotiations.' His little voice is quivering even more and a few sobs slip out with every few words. He used the back of his little hand to wipe his nose. The worst part is that we know poor Max hasn't got a clue about what he is saying and this little boy, who is so innocent, is being used as a bargaining chip just because his father is the UK's prime minister. He looks up to the man standing next to him to see if what he has said is correct. The man nods his head. I feel the tears streaming down my face. I am wondering how much more time they will give the British government. Surely a few more days is all it will take to get things organised for the British Intelligence to track them down.

He says again, 'ISIS has been trying to negotiate for weeks but the British Intelligence keeps on moving the deadline, saying they need more time. There is no more time.' One of the fighters takes Max by the shoulder and pulls him in front of the table. They make Max kneel in front and all the men stand forward in a half-circle around him. I'm thinking surely they aren't going to hurt an innocent child. I have seen these scenes before on the news when they have captured people and behead them to make a statement. There is a large black flag with Arabic writing in white all over it. They put the blindfold over his eyes. I'm thinking, *ok, they are going to march him out of the room*. Then they start chanting *Allahu Akbar, Allahu Akbar, Allahu Akbar* with raised fists. It happens so quickly that I don't even have time to react. The knifeman pulls up Max's head and, within what feels like a hundredth of a second, slides the knife across his throat. Blood splatters everywhere and Max's body jerks and just becomes limp. It happened so quickly I don't even have time to shut my eyes. The knifeman is still holding onto his head and you can see inside his neck as it is sliced open. He lets go of the head and the body falls over. It now seems to be happening in slow motion. He steps over Max's body and walks towards the camera and turns it off. As fast as that happened, I hear myself scream and throw up at the same time. Yaz hears me and runs into the room.

'Mummy! Are you ok? Why are you screaming?'

I push her out of the room as I run to the bathroom to continue throwing up. I only have one hand to guide her out with as the other one is holding up my t-shirt. It is all down the front of my t-shirt as it was the only thing I could think of to pull up and catch the sick in.

Yaz starts to cry, 'Mummy what's going on, why you are getting sick? Mummy, you are scaring me!'

I tell her not to worry, I think I have eaten too much. I tell her to go back into her room as I don't want her going into the lounge. I know there will be reruns all day and I don't want her near the television without me being in the room. I rip my clothes off and have a quick shower. I brush my teeth and wrap myself in a towel and go back into the lounge. I don't even get dressed.

Back in the studio, I see Huw Edwards. He looks ill and you can see he is struggling to hold back the tears. He says they will be going back over to 10 Downing Street as the Deputy Prime Minister will be issuing a statement. They go over to Number 10 to see what the mood is like outside and the correspondent is very professional, but his voice is trembling as he speaks. A policeman comes out and says they will be issuing a statement in an hour's time. They go back live to the studio. There is a photo of Max in the background, a happy boy whose life was cut so short by barbarians.

I stare at the telly and wonder if everyone in the studio is thinking the same as me, was that real or was it all a staged set-up and hopefully Max will appear any moment with them saying something along the lines of, 'Next time it is for real.'

I ask myself how a human being can be filled with so much hatred that they can kill a child who has never done evil and justify it in the name of religion. Would Allah allow this? I know not. I always had a fascination with different religions and Islam in particular. I did read up on it and read the Majestic Quran and looked at different quotes and all of them say how Allah loves all. We all know Allah/God is the same in all religions and he is a loving, merciful God. I think about one of the quotes I read by the Prophet Muhammad (PBUH) that said: 'Whoever kills a Mu'ahid (a person who is granted the pledge of protection by the Muslims) shall not smell the fragrance of Paradise though its fragrance can be smelt at a distance of forty years (of travelling).'

I get dressed and then go to the kitchen to fetch disinfectant and old tea towels and start cleaning the floor. As I pray, I call out to God, 'Why? Why are there people with such hatred in their hearts?' I think of those innocent people they have beheaded, executed, drowned or burnt alive and pray that God will never allow them to enter heaven. What animals? Who beheads a child live on television? These people are filled with Satan as there is no way they can be doing this in the name of religion. Vakkas always said when Muslims start to do evil like this, then we are to know they aren't Muslims and don't follow the Qur'an. He said, 'They will never enter paradise, but at the end of the day it is

Allah's decision who goes to heaven and who doesn't. We are servants and Allah will decide. '

CHAPTER SEVEN

The world is condemning the actions of ISIS and calling for retaliation. These are definitely of the worst kind of atrocities along with the Holocaust to happen. I do remember 9/11 vividly as I was living in Boston at the time and Logon Airport was so upset as two planes flew from the Airport and I think they will never forgive themselves for allowing those men to breach security. They weren't flagged as dangerous, so of course, they passed security checks.

The newsreaders are in tears as they talk about the beheading of Max. I can't imagine a more difficult moment for anyone. You need to be professional, yet you are talking about a beautiful boy who was beheaded live on television and not to cry is just not possible. I hear his name and I start crying. The cameras are on Downing Street and the Deputy Prime Minister comes and says they will be issuing a formal statement in due course. They keep on extending the time, I don't blame them; if my son had been beheaded there is no way I would be able to make a statement. He asks for prayers and asks that we give the Prime Minister and his family time to grieve. They are in utter disbelief and the pain is unbearable. For a family to see their only child murdered live on television is beyond words. To know someone's brief life on earth can end in such a painful way has devastated them so much.

A couple of hours later the Prime Minster appears, which is a shock as we were all expecting the Deputy Prime Minister to be making the statement. His eye are very swollen from all the crying. He starts by saying, 'Max radiated all good things. He loved everyone, never discriminated and was kind, caring and giving. He was a child who respected others and believed in everyone. He always saw the good in others and was very quick to challenge you if he saw that you didn't treat others with respect. We always joked he would be a prime minister one day as well.' He pauses and then carries on, 'Today the world will grieve as a family, we will become one nation through Max's life.' He turns around and walks back into Number 10. You can see the cameras' flashes going off and you can hear voices shouting out. It's not the usual shouts of one question or "just a moment, *Prime Minister*", the shouts are "*we are with you and we are praying for you*".

They return to the studio and announce that the rest of the day will be a mixture of movies, interviews and news reports and they will not be following the usual schedule. I presume no one really wants to be in front of the camera and would prefer a load of reruns playing instead of having to keep the British-stiff upper lip.

Later on, in the evening, the news shows different groups of people gathering in parks and other open spaces having vigils for Max. It reminds me of the time when Princess Diana died. Everywhere there are groups of people sitting, lighting candles either praying or meditating. Yaz and I get back into our usual Sunday night routine, making sure her school bag is packed, her uniform is clean, PE bag has everything in it and her homework is done. She bathes reads a bit and goes to bed. I watch the news and decide to have a bath as well. I lie in the bathtub crying uncontrollably and feel exhausted after a while. I go to bed as I really can't be bothered to do anything else.

The next morning, after dropping Yaz off at school, I put the telly on before going to work. Downing Street has had to call in extra security as people are leaving flowers. People have now started leaving the flowers by the statue of the Earl of Mountbatten. So overnight thousands of bouquets have appeared. They say the police will distribute them to care homes and hospitals. I'm wondering how his parents will get Max's body back to bury him or will ISIS throw his body out with the rest of the prisoners they have killed. I have never actually thought about this before. What does happen to the bodies? Will the Prime Minister have to start negotiating to get Max's body back? I cannot imagine the pain of having to negotiate to get your child's body back so you can say goodbye to him and feel like for the last time, you will be putting him somewhere safe. I've never wanted to be buried, I've always wanted to be cremated and have my ashes set free so my soul can rise up to the Lord. I want them to float up to heaven and help me to be able to sit at Jesus' feet one day, I sound like some sort of nutter. I have signed a donor's card, so I make sure I am healthy so I can donate as much of my body to save as many lives as possible.

The BBC announces that the Queen will be saying something in 15 minutes time. I sit waiting for her and those are a long 15 minutes. I realise I might be late for work but think it's worth it, I'll not take lunch to make up the time.

It is amazing how the nation has changed its views on her in recent years. She went through a stage of being one of the most disliked royals to being one of the favourites. The little piece she played in the Olympics was so good, I still occasionally watch it on YouTube. She comes on and she is sitting on a sofa. She talks about her heartache for the Prime Minister and how she knew Max and he was one of the loveliest children she ever met. So polite and considerate. She talks about how we as a nation must not give into hatred and love our neighbours as we love ourselves. She is a true Christian and I love the fact she never shies away from it. She is happy to admit she loves the Lord and is happy to say *"let's pray for each other"*. I am also glad to see the younger royals all go to church. It is so important for a nation, who is supposedly Christian, to appreciate that the church is for all ages, unlike these politicians who are agnostic or don't practise any religion. Seriously, have the balls to either believe or be an atheist, don't sit on the fence and be agnostic.

It has been announced that the Prime Minister will be releasing a statement at 9pm tonight. My heart really aches for the family. Facebook and Instagram are flooded with those little sayings of *"tell family and friends you love them, hug a loved one* and *don't stay angry, your life can change in an instant"* etc. Everyone now has a photo of Max. All of a sudden you have these parents who a few months ago were saying *"my little shit is so annoying* or *can't wait for him or her to leave home"*, now they sing a different tune. *"My little so and so is my life"* and *"I live for my kids, holding them extra close today."* How something like this can change our outlook on life. Life changes in an instant.

Later on I am sitting on the sofa with a hot water bottle, a cup of hot chocolate and waiting for the old familiar jingle of the BBC news to come on and I'm feeling anxious.

CHAPTER EIGHT

'Good evening and welcome to this special edition of this evening's news. We will be going directly to Downing Street,' a very short introduction by the newsreader.

The Prime Minister is sitting behind a desk and you can see he is in agony having to issue this statement. It's the first time I have seen the Prime Minister sit behind a desk to deliver a speech; I can't blame him. My legs would buckle if I had to talk about my child's gruesome death in front of millions of people.

'Good evening and on behalf of myself and my wife, we would like to thank you all for the prayers, cards and flowers. Your love has been overwhelming and is helping us in the most difficult time of our lives. No parent wants to outlive their child and no parent wants to see their child die the most horrific and gruesome death.' He is so pale and tiny beads of sweat seem to be appearing. He stops to take a drink of water and breathes slowly for a few minutes before continuing. 'I cannot begin to tell you the pain we are experiencing, it's excruciating. To see your most beautiful boy beheaded live on television is barbaric and beyond comprehension. Max gave us so much joy, his infectious laugh, his inquisitiveness, his love for life and he always saw the good in others. He loved helping people he said it was his gift from God. It was so cute when we would get visitors over, he always wanted to pour the tea and handout the cake and biscuits. I can add that many of those cakes or biscuits Max helped bake.' He stops to breathe again, and I can see his eyes starting to tear up. He takes a hanky out of his pocket and wipes his eyes. He takes another sip of water. He seems frozen as he sits so still for a minute to compose himself. I feel the tears run down my cheeks.

'On April 27th Max had been invited to a birthday party of a friend. He really wanted to go as there was going to be a sundae-building competition.' The Prime Minister give a small smile. 'Max was beside himself with excitement, he even started sketching the different layers he was going to build to make sure his was the best. He even wanted us to have a practice run at home, no flies on him. As Max was best friends with the birthday boy, he thought he had inside knowledge of all the sweets that were going to be bought and all the syrups etc. Little did he know that everyone was having input on the sweets as well. The two apparently plotted and made a list of things his mum needed to buy to make the ultimate sundaes.'

The party was of a boy in Max's class, they were really good friends, as I said earlier more like best friends. The family, mum, dad and his best friend was from Iran, both parents were doctors at St Thomas' and also, we felt it was very important that Max went to the party as we wanted to show how important it is to us as a family that everyone feels welcome in this country and is accepted. Besides, there was no chance of us not allowing Max to go as the sundae-building contest was the talk of the class. Max did not want to miss out on it. He came home very excited as each child was given a list of the ice creams and toppings so if there were any allergies they could be removed. This list was put up on the fridge with a magnet and Max was constantly looking at the list to remind himself of his winning combo. Like most parents, we did not allow a lot of unhealthy snacks, sweets etc. at home. So, you can imagine Max was dreaming about this competition.' The Prime Minister has a little smile on his face before he continues.

'The family arrived in the UK a couple of years ago. Max said he knew his friend didn't have a lot of British toys, so he wanted him to have a sort of keepsake gift as they were still new to the UK. Max chose a beautiful popup book of London and wrote the loveliest message inside of it. He also wanted a fun gift, so we bought some traditional British cars and buses. Apparently, books aren't a real gift.

Max was accompanied to the party by one bodyguard,' he added.

He stops again and drinks some more water. He sits quietly for a moment.

'Everything went well. There were a lot of children at the party, probably around 35 children. The bodyguard said the ice cream sundae contest went off without a hitch and Max won first prize. We were not surprised considering the way that boy practised, sketched etc., he could have written a book on ice cream sundaes. He won a pretend gold medal and a large box of chocolates. That's heaven for any 11-year-old. Apparently, he was ecstatic and wore the medal with pride and a few ice creams stains on his t-shirt. After half an hour or so Max started to complain of a stomach-ache. His friend's mum told the bodyguard she would take him into her office and give him something to stop the pain and settle his tummy. Apparently, she just laughed and said he probably over did it with all the junk food. I want you to understand the reason I am saying "bodyguard" is because I want to protect this man who loved Max with all his heart and saw him grow up. We have a team of bodyguards and I feel it is important they know they aren't to blame and need to be protected. He is living in hell since this happened and blames himself. You have to know what this organisation did, the meticulous planning and it was done over a period of time and not just a random act. There was no way of stopping them even if there were ten bodyguards.'

The bodyguard said the mum took Max into her office and came out and claimed she had convinced Max to get some rest for a few minutes. She apparently gave him something to settle his stomach and said it needed ten minutes to work. The bodyguard said he popped his head in and Max was lying on a large sofa. He smiled and waved. She offered the bodyguard coffee and some birthday cake and said that she would fetch Max from the office once his stomach had settled. She winked and said he'll be able to face round two of cake and pizza. The bodyguard said he looked at Max and his face lit up when he heard the words cake and pizza. They had a little chuckle and she shut the door. She asked the guard if he wanted to sit in the lounge away from the children to have five minutes of peace. He walked past the kitchen/conservatory and the other children were watching a show with some magician making balloon animals.

The doctor called her son and said he should pop his head in to see if Max is ok. She called her husband who walked with the bodyguard to the lounge and said she would be back in five minutes. The bodyguard said nothing seemed strange or out of the ordinary. Remember these men are highly trained and can pick on the smallest of details. They went into the lounge, chatted for a few minutes. She came in a little while later and joined them and the three had coffee and birthday cake. He said they were really a lovely couple, easy to talk to and very hospitable and that he could hear the laughter of the other children having a wonderful time. Suddenly, his head felt a bit strange and the doctor asked him if he felt okay.

He tried to stand up and the next thing he knew he was being carried out on a stretcher into an ambulance.'

The Prime Minister stops talking for a few minutes. I can imagine the whole nation sitting in silence waiting for him to start up again. 'What MI5 can make out is that Max was drugged with something very effective that knocked him out in the five minutes. This gave her time to talk to Max and her son, who we presume was also given something to put him to sleep. The couple, together with their son and Max, left by a side door and were driven away to London City Airport. The reason we think she must have drugged their own son it is because it would have been difficult for him to leave his own party without kicking up a fuss and I think seeing his best friend carried out would cause a problem. We are still working on a timeline. No evidence of drugs was left behind. Blood has been taken from the bodyguard and tests have been carried out to determine what drug was used. There must have been a team of helpers getting them into the getaway cars. As the police searched the property, they found it was left completely furnished. It is as if they have popped out for the day, even leaving behind all the birthday gifts. The neighbours noticed a couple of black Range Rovers but being central London and an elite neighbourhood, no one really takes any notice as most people own expensive cars. We believe Max was put into some crate with oxygen and loaded onto the plane. It appears no one actually noticed for a while as the magician kept all the children entertained. There were a few hired helpers there, and they carried on as normal looking after the children. The Doctors told the girls who were hired to help clean up at the beginning of the party that if they disappeared for a little while it was because they have a few patients they need to talk to. One of the girls recalls them laughing and saying, " doctors never have a day off." 'This plot was extremely well orchestrated and very meticulously planned,' the Prime Minister states.

He takes another breather and you can see he is in such pain making this statement.

He continues, 'Parents started arriving and they noticed that the birthday boy wasn't around either. One of the helpers went and knocked on the office door and there was no answer. She said she left it as she thought maybe they were on calls with patients, and she didn't want to interrupt them. She presumed Max still wasn't feeling well and their son was keeping him company. As it was so quiet, she thought maybe they had moved Max upstairs. Being in the kitchen/conservatory on the other side of the house with 30+ children they couldn't hear anything. Hyperactive children who overdosed on sweets, ice cream, fizzy drinks etc. can make enough noise to drown out a brass band.

The girls from the catering company started handing out the party bags and told everyone that the doctors were on call with patients and that the birthday boy was probably sitting with Max who overdid it on ice cream. Parents and children were happy with the explanation and left. As parents arrived sporadically and then stood around chatting, eating cake, pizza and sweets it must have added another half an hour on before they managed to get rid of everyone. They started clearing up thinking that any moment the doctors would appear and they would be told they could go home. The magician left saying he had already been paid in advance. One of the girls from the catering company decided to have a little look around the house in case a child had popped into one of the other rooms and left cake or sweets and they wanted to tidy up everything. They had also been paid in advance and the girls said they were not only given a really good tip, they also saw there were party bags for each of them with lovely toiletries, expensive chocolates and candles. So, they were more than happy to make sure everything was tidied up nicely. One of the girls opened one of the doors downstairs to the lounge. She noticed cups and cake and ventured inside to fetch them so she could load them into the dishwasher. She said that is when she noticed legs sticking out from behind a large coffee table and when she went over, she realised it was the bodyguard lying on the floor. She said she ran over to him, but he wasn't moving. She called to the others. One ran to fetch the doctors. She knocked and again no answer. She opened the door and saw no one was around. She ran upstairs and couldn't find anyone. It never even crossed her mind that something was wrong. She presumed the bodyguard just fainted and the doctors would be able to help him. She ran downstairs and one of the other girls said they couldn't find Max, then panic set in. They split up and started frantically running around the house and garden and found no one was there. One of the girls from the catering company rang for an ambulance and one rang the police and told them that they were at the party and the prime minister's son was missing. In a matter of minutes there were police all over the place.' He stops for another minute to compose himself and while doing so plays with his wedding band. 'MI5 suggested that they could have left up to two hours before and, with everything going on and so many children, no one noticed.

We found out that four private planes left from London City Airport and in each were four adults and a child. They had three decoy planes to different destinations. The diversions caused a delay in finding the real plane. One of the planes went to France, one to Turkey, another to Spain and the fourth to Russia. We believe Max was on the plane that flew to Turkey where they got onto a different plane and flew to Syria. Getting this information and being able to track them down, unfortunately, didn't happen as quickly as we hoped and by then the plane had already landed in Syria and they were beyond reach'.

'We understand the couple came to the UK two years ago and started working at St Thomas' Hospital. St Thomas' Hospital is renowned for its medical treatments all over the world. They can choose from the best of the best in medical staff. So obviously they were very well checked and passed security clearance without any difficulties. They enrolled their son into the same school and class as Max. From the intelligence we have received and working on different theories it appears ISIS has been working on this plan for at least four years. ISIS had gone through a lot of trouble finding the perfect couple with a son of the same age as Max. They also had to find the decoy families who were willing to be arrested if need be. The meticulous details are exceptional,' he adds.

'The two boys quickly became friends, having playdates and sleepovers. We accepted the family into our home and had them over for barbeques and dinners. We even invited them to a garden party at Buckingham Palace. The boys became inseparable. I want to add, British intelligence had done a thorough background check on the family. They seemed to be a normal, wealthy family that left Iran to improve their lives, give their son a chance to receive a better education and to live a freer life. The hospital only has praise for their work ethics, their kindness and compassion to patients. They were model citizens, and they were truly loved and respected by their colleagues.' He stops talking again and after wiping his nose starts up.

'When the staff were interviewed, they said that sometimes in the holidays their son would come into the hospital and have lunch with his parents. He was so polite and well-spoken. Whenever he came to meet his parents for lunch he would bring little treats for the nurses and doctors, sometimes packets of biscuits or bags of sweets. What a remarkable young man? I wonder what will happen to him now,' the Prime Minister says. He pauses once again and I wonder if he is thinking about their son and how his life has changed in an instant as well. He resumes, 'They were a very giving family as the other consultants said the couple loved bringing in little treats for the staff as well, especially on Friday. They would bring in cakes to enjoy as the last day of the week and to wish everyone a Jummah Mubarak, which is a special day for Muslims. They would have a lunch break and listen to a *khutbah*, which is a sermon read out in the mosque by the imam. They would listen out for the *adhan* and then they would pray in one of their colleagues' offices that wasn't in use, but they never made a big thing out of it. You must remember a very high percentage of doctors are Muslims so praying is nothing out of the ordinary. I am told they rarely went to the communal prayer room to pray, as it was on the other side of the hospital and it was much faster to just pray wherever they were. The staff mentioned they were so hardworking, putting in twice the effort as any of the other doctors. They made everyone feel loved and special. When the staff remark how they greet the cleaners with the same respect they showed everyone else and nothing was too difficult for them, then you know they are good people, yet I cannot understand why they would do this to Max? They took him into their home, fed him, had days out together knowing all along they were going to kidnap him and ultimately see him sacrificed.' He stops and it is as if he hears these words for the first time and it hits him so hard that he gasps for breath. My heart aches seeing him in such agony.

'According to the other staff they were always first in and last to leave. The patients loved them, they had such a special way with their patients.' He takes a bottle of water and sits very still for a minute. He looks like he needs a little bit of time to compose himself again. He sips the water slowly before he continues.

'We now believe they were getting teachings directly from ISIS. Their last day at work they left as usual, wishing everyone a lovely weekend and went home. We know now everything about them was fake, the only thing we can work out is that they are real doctors, but name-wise we don't know. ISIS gave them new identities with false passports.'

My mind drifts and I wonder if they will miss this amazing life they seemed to have in the UK. I wonder if they hated the thought of having to give it all up to go back to treating wounded fighters. They had to give up a beautiful home and an amazing school for their son. I wouldn't be able to do it. They must be really dedicated to ISIS and the cause it stands for.

****

Raqqa is going to be so difficult to live in. I read there aren't supermarkets you can pop into to get supplies or coffee shops where you can meet your friends. I hear the people of Raqqa are trying to rebuild the city and move on but it is still a large city covered in ruins or building riddled with bullet holes. The main roundabouts were where they held executions or chopped off people's limbs. The inhabitants of Raqqa have destroyed the buildings that were used for Sharia courts or passport offices by ISIS. They are trying to push ISIS out but my understanding is that there are still a lot of ISIS supporters. They want to get rid of anything associated with ISIS. I hear the prime minister clear his throat and I start listening to him speaking. 'We received a phone call very late in the evening saying they had Max and they wanted a prisoner swap. Without going into a lot of detail we said we needed time as these are extremely high-ranking leaders in ISIS who have orchestrated the deaths of thousands and it isn't possible to agree to something like this so quickly. We realised that Max was probably in Syria by now. By the way, the passengers in the other three other planes have been detained and British intelligence went to the respective countries to arrest them and bring them back to the UK. They claim to be wealthy families going on holiday. They aren't on the list of extremists and have never raised any suspicion. They are British families, so no suspicion was raised.' He takes another sip of water, stops and then drinks a few more sips and wipes his mouth with his hand. It is as if he has forgotten for a split second where he is.

He then says, 'We are now only speculating the doctors are in hiding before they will emerge using their real identities. They will be working full time for ISIS again. My heart does go out to their son who just like Max is innocent and caught up in such atrocities.' Saying his son's name must really hurt. I can see his eyes start to tear up. He takes another sip of water, breathes and you can see his chest rise up and go down again. 'At this time this is all I am at liberty to share with you but when we get any more information, I will update you. I ask that you please keep us in your prayers, pray for one another and, most of all, love one another. Thank you and good night.'

The broadcast ends with some rolling footage of Max. So devastating that he had to give his little life for something that never had anything to do with him. As the Muslims believe, it was his time and he will have eternal life.

I sit for a few moments and think, *"Well it's back to being covered in black and having your life ruled by extremists."* Their whole routine is dictated to them. Yet when I think of Islam, I always think of peaceful, kind and caring people. To me, they are beautiful people and not evil as we see on television. Amazing how a group within a group can be so radically different. Well I suppose you only need to look at the Christians, there must be thousands of different types of churches and all of them think they are the right religion.

CHAPTER NINE

The shock of Max's death hasn't worn off yet and to sit here listening to what they did to orchestrate this whole thing is unbelievable, just like the planning of the Twin Towers. Who sits there planning the deaths of thousands of people thinking it is ok and you will enter paradise one day? Think about it, who sits there saying: *"I have a brilliant idea, let's fly planes into the World Trade Centre simultaneously and kill thousands of innocent people, even Muslims."* Thank goodness God is in control and if the one plane hadn't been delayed, they would have killed thousands more. We can be so grateful God had his hand in that situation.

This is like a James Bond movie coming alive. It seems unreal; the kind of people they are able to recruit or who seem to sign up with them. Seriously, how does anyone even sign up to an organisation like this? What would you google, *"How to join ISIS?"* Is there a contact number, application form or office address? I thought when people searched for this kind of stuff, it was supposed to send messages to the CIA or whoever looks out for terrorists. Maybe that's why it is probably so much easier to recruit through different local groups and even some mosques. Everyone knows there are certain mosques that are able to radicalise people and get them to join ISIS.

It seems like many young people have joined and are willing to lay down their lives for the cause. It seems like an ideology that has gained stardom. The cool thing to belong to. Young girls are running off to marry fighters, to be the lovely wife they can come home to after a long day in battle, have babies to carry on with the ideology. The community of living, eating and praying together like normal people. So what makes a 15-year-old convince her friends to run off with her to Syria?

When I think of community living, I think of the kibbutz in Israel. I used to live in one and it was the most amazing community life. We ate three meals a day together, went off to work and shared everything. If someone got a bag of peaches, they would share them with their neighbours, I was invited every Friday for a Shabbat tea by a man called David, with a friend called Monique. Mo and I lived for Fridays; we would eat so much that we could never have dinner. We would have sandwiches, veg sticks and dips and always some delicious cake. I actually returned a few months after I left as I missed the community life so much and went back to my routine of having afternoon tea with David on a Friday. The only difference with the kibbutz I lived on and that of ISIS is that here they don't ask you to take up weapons and kill people; they plant orange trees, slight difference.

If I was half as devoted a Christian, I would never have to worry about not sitting at Jesus' feet one day. As Christians, we all long for eternal life and it isn't easy living with the worldly temptations around us. When I mention I'm a Christian, people around me smile, I can see how uncomfortable they start to feel. A lot of people like to think of themselves as Christian in the UK, but most don't have any connection to a church. It is very rare that I'll meet someone who says, "So am I" I have to be honest, I find most Christians very judgemental and as I always say, most Christians are very unchristian. They are very happy to take but don't like to give in return. I have had so many people over for meals and, hand on my heart, 99% of these so-called Christians never invited me into their homes.

There is something magical about Islam. Some people admire it from afar, we would never be brave enough to walk into a mosque and start asking questions. You know us British (well, I am now British although I was born in South Africa), we don't like to do something that might make us a little bit uncomfortable. We never want to question anything or seem politically incorrect.

Mosque's for Muslims are more than a place to go and pray. It is the centrality of the Muslim community life, so it is logical that violent extremists have tried to exploit mosques as a place in which to find support and recruit followers. I remember hearing the Finsbury Park Mosque was once described as an al-Qaeda guesthouse in London. It assisted in the radicalisation of Zacarias Moussaoui, one of the 9/11 plotters. Abu Hamza, the radical imam, the hook-handed preacher of hate, used to preach at the Finsbury Park Mosque and he turned out a generation of militants willing to die or kill for their cause. What drives two extremely intelligent people who have come from privileged families to join an organisation like ISIS? These are doctors who took the Hippocratic Oath to save lives. How do you radicalise someone that they are prepared to kill an innocent child? As parents, we do whatever it takes to protect our children and even other children. It is a natural instinct to want to protect the innocent. Every day the news releases statements and updating the world on their findings. They are obviously fed drips and drabs from British intelligence. It seems these doctors are very high up in the ranks at ISIS. They lived in a large house and it seems the owner is an imam from the Finsbury Park Mosque, small world. Slowly the pieces of the puzzle are starting to fit.

CHAPTER TEN

Living on the high street in a small village you hear a lot. I hear screaming late one night and look out the window. I'm across the road from a takeaway pizza place run by guys from Iran, Afghanistan, Pakistan and Turkey. They have all been in the country for years. I think the pizza place has been open for 15 or more years. Most have worked there since the opening. A few troublemakers have turned up and have started harassing the guys. They try telling the attackers they aren't ISIS members, but they aren't listening. I decide to go over the road to give my support, thinking if a woman is standing there the troublemakers might leave. I know the people in the pizzeria well, occasionally when they are short-staffed, I help out by answering the phone and taking orders. They never pay me; they give me the odd pizza so it works out well for all of us. I pop over the road and a crowd is already gathering. The three drunks are swearing and shouting and accusing them of killing Max. A few people step in and tell them to back off and leave the guys alone. One of the drunks is sitting on the wall having a cigarette, he finds a brick and throws it at one of the guys and cuts his arm open. Two of the men tackle him down and call 999. A few more people call 999 so it doesn't take long for the police to arrive. The poor pizza guy is bundled inside and his friends help him clean up the wound. He refuses to go to the hospital. I go inside and ask if they need anything. They are very polite and say they are alright and don't need any help and then start shouting in whatever language they speak I haven't got a clue. They become very loud and animated when explaining something and everyone talks at the same time. The police stand talking to the drunks for about half an hour and send them on their way. They caution them and say any more trouble they will be arrested. I'm appalled they didn't arrest the guy that threw the brick, it could have been a lot worse. It is a hate crime after all. They say they can't arrest him. It's more like they can't be bothered as it means paperwork. Stonesfield has the worst police. They are known for their laziness and bad work ethics. I have seen a woman run out of a shop with things she stole, and the policeman watched her run away as he couldn't be bothered to chase after her. When questioned he said, 'I'm not risking my life for a few blouses and she is too fast anyway.' What a terrible attitude the police have in trying to apprehend criminals. They can't even be bothered to put in any effort to catch criminals. She'll be back tomorrow and the day after as she knows nothing is going to happen to her and the shop will have a financial loss. I stand talking to the pizza guys and it is so sad to see innocent people being harassed just because they are Muslim and now tarnished with the same brush.

I phone my vicar and tell him we really need to contact the mosque to see if there is anything we can help them with. Our church has built up a very good relationship with the mosque. Every year we have a football match of Christians versus Muslims and it is one of the best days in Stonesfield. We all take food and sit around afterwards, eat together and have a fun day out. There are two matches, the main game and then the over 60's walking football match. That is hilarious, they are only allowed to walk to the ball, so no chance of injuries or heart attacks. We always talk about how good looking the Muslim guys are, so there is always a good crowd to support the match.

My friend Cathy always says, 'God is so good, I got to be stationed just outside where the Muslim guys are playing, definitely so easy on the eye.'

I teased her, 'Really Cathy, you always make sure you sit in the same place every year and every year you tell me how good God is to you.' We laugh.

We also have weekly catch-ups with the Muslim women, a coffee morning every Tuesday and the women have arranged a pudding evening to raise funds for Syrian refugees. Cliff phones me the next day to tell me he spoke to the Imam and they have been having a lot of trouble. There are groups of people turning up outside at Friday prayers and they are harassing the men who go for prayers. When they try and drive through to the back where the parking spaces and entrance are, they say things are being thrown at them. We decide we need to get a group of strong Christian men together and they need to go on a Friday and form a barrier so the Muslim men can go and pray in peace. The imam is really grateful and tells Cliff that people have been turning up at his house. They have followed his wife and children home and are constantly banging on the door. They are pushing things through the letterbox. It has got to the stage where he now sleeps by the front door as one night someone pushed burning paper through the letterbox. It is heart-breaking to hear this, what has the world got to?

'I think we need to find them a safe house. Cliff can you send out an emergency email as we have a lot of wealthy people in our church and people who own more than one property, maybe they can let the imam and his family stay there for a few weeks?", I ask him.

We agree it is no use them moving in with another Muslim family as they will also be harassed. It will just be a continuous process of harassment from one family to the next. They have removed their children from the local school as they are scared other children will start bullying them. Our prayers have been answered as one of the families has an apartment they have just decorated and waiting for the local estate agents to find them tenants. We decided we need to move quickly and the following evening, under the cover of darkness, well 10pm to be exact, a group of us arrive at the imam's house and help them pack up essentials. I have grabbed a few empty suitcases from home and so did everyone else. We got boxes and tape from the local One-Stop. We hire two vans from the local 24/7 hire company and a mixed group of Christians and Muslims meet up at the house to start packing and moving the essential pieces of furniture. I'm here to help Basheera, the imam's wife gets as much of the children's toys and clothes together. We want it to be home away from home for them. There might be days where they will be staying indoors all day, so we need to make sure they have things to keep them entertained. The men are there to help move furniture. They just need basic things like beds, sofas and the dining table. We have to move as swiftly and quietly as possible. They park the vans around the corner and quietly start packing up as much stuff as possible. The plan is to get everything boxed up and once that it done they will load the vans. The men line up the furniture, getting it all ready for when the vans arrive so that they can load it on as quickly as possible.

Basheera starts to cry saying, 'I would never have thought we would have to leave our house in the middle of the night in Stonesfield. We thought when we were asked to move here, that it was a village with well-educated people close to Oxford, diverse and we would be accepted. We never ever feared for our lives.'

I really feel for her, as a foreigner myself I know that you never really get accepted. There are a few people in Stonesfield who accept outsiders. I try and comfort her as much as possible and suggest we have a little break with some tea and cake I bought along. We start brewing and handing out mugs of tea and offering the cake to everyone around. I was introduced to a few of the other men helping. A young guy walks in with a really witty sense of humour who I warm to straight away. I don't really see him doing much carrying, apparently, he is there to give moral support. Everyone is teasing him saying he just goes from one room to the next talking and carrying the odd box. He laughs and says he is there to make sure everyone isn't getting stressed. 'I'm a COO I don't actually get my hands dirty, I get other people do to the work,' he says. The other guys laugh and throw pillows at him.

Basheera calls him over and introduces me to him. She says, 'Sarah let me introduce you to Abdul, another member from the mosque and has really good knowledge of the Qur'an, he will be able to answer all your questions on Islam. He has a wonderful brain, Masha 'Allah'. She guides him over towards me, 'Abdul, come and meet Sarah. We go to the women's weekly meetings where the Christian and Muslim women meet up. Sarah is really interested in learning more about Islam. She was born into a Jewish Orthodox family and when she moved to America she converted to Christianity.'

'Oh, really and now you will become a Muslim and find the right path, third time lucky,' he says and then adds, 'You won't even have to change your name as you have Prophet Ibrahim's wife's name, Masha 'Allah.' 'Well I don't want to convert; I just want to learn more about Islam as I find it fascinating and I feel it is really similar to the Jewish religion,' I say. 'As a child, I grew up in rural South Africa and the village I lived in was predominately Dutch Reformed or Afrikaans people. There were a few Jewish families and quite a few families from India and Pakistan. On Fridays, a siren would go off and you could see all the men kicking off their flip flops and running to the mosque. I thought it was so amazing how devoted they were. Then later on in the evening, all the Jewish families would walk to the synagogue. We would go Saturday mornings again and then our Sabbath ended in the evening,' I rambled on. 'I just feel it is important to learn from one another,' I say again.

Abdul stares at me for a moment and then says, 'You know when you convert to Islam you form a personal and direct relationship with God by worshipping Him alone, without the need of intermediaries. One feels this personal relationship and is aware that God knows everything and is there to assist you. Believe that the Judgment Day is true and will come. Do not worship anything nor anyone except God.'

I reply, 'That is the same with being Jewish and Christian, so our religions aren't different, but very similar actually.' Abdul reminds me that the Christians believe in the trinity and don't worship God alone. There is also thousands of different types of churches he says and all have their own reading that they follow. The Bible has also been written into so many different versions where the Qur'an has never been changed and if you are in London or Shanghai you read exactly the same words and it's the same as what the Prophet Mohammad (PBUH) read. The Qur'an has never been rewritten with different interpretations. I find that amazing and share my impression.

He laughs and says, 'Thinking about it, what you need to do is take time off work and spend the next few months just studying Islam. Forget about work, friends etc. Give 100% of your time to understand it and then decide if you want to convert to Islam. Do you know that in our religion you can convert on your own, but it is much better to do it with the help of someone from the mosque just to aid you with your newfound faith?' Abdul stares at me for a moment and then adds, 'Do you know the word Muslim means one who submits to the will of God, regardless of his or her race, nationality or ethnic background, so my love, you can become a Muslim, we don't discriminate.'

Basheera adds, 'I told you, he has such good knowledge of Islam and he is a very successful and extremely young COO of a housing association. A young man in demand over here. All the women here with daughters want him as a son-in-law.'

Abdul laughs, 'I'm married to my work and way too young to settle down. Anyway, my mum has someone in mind already, and I know what's good for me so I'll marry my mum's choice, or will I?' He winks at me and laughs.

'So, Abdul, as much as I am impressed with you being in demand, I am more interested in my salvation. So, let's get back to why you think I need to convert so quickly?' I ask amused. 'Why do I need to study 24/7 and do it so intensely and hastily? Do you have a direct connection to Allah and know that the world is going to end soon?'

He laughs and says, 'No, of course I don't, but I'm thinking when ISIS finds out a Jew has converted to Islam, you'll be the next one on the telly getting your head sliced off, but you'll be a Muslim at least so you'll enter paradise.' This boy has such a warped sense of humour but a very warm personality. 'Jokes aside, we Muslims love Jews, most of the prophets come from the Old Testament and we love the Prophet Jesus. Do you know

Mary, his mother, is the most respected woman in the Qur'an, she is actually the only woman named in the Qur'an?' he tells me.

That really is amazing, somehow I thought they hated any other religion. He adds, 'We say in Islam you can't be a real Muslim unless you love Jesus, all other religions and prophets."

I now ask, 'Do you think I'll get to heaven or as you call it paradise?' 'The greatest benefit is that a Muslim is promised by God the reward of eternal Paradise. Those who are blessed with Paradise will live eternally in bliss without any sort of sickness, pain or sadness.'

'Let's meet and I'll explain everything to you, I won't hide anything and I will answer all your questions about Islam. It is important to hear it from a Muslim and not a book as I can tell you the truth and explain things in more detail and I know then I will make you a Muslim. I feel you are searching for true religion and if you give me a chance, I will show you. Jokes aside, I need to introduce you to a good friend of mine, her name is Tanvi. She is a good egg, actually thinking about it, she knows jack shit about Islam, but you'll never meet a nicer person.'

We laugh and start chatting about how similar our religions are and just how fascinating it is that we all want to serve God. It is so lovely to meet people who are proud to serve God and never shy away from showing their love to Him. As Abdul says we all serve one God, just that he is called different names.

I say, 'You know Abdul, it doesn't matter which religion you follow, it seems we all want to have eternal life one day and the only way is through God.'

'So true, life is temporary. We go through the same things every day. Rich or poor, we all have a routine but we need to do this and live our lives with God knowing we will see eternal life one day,' he says.

The others start shouting at us in joking voices that we need to stop talking and start working. We laugh and get back to work.

We load the vans up quickly in the early hours of the morning and go and unpack them at the flat in the centre of town. Basheera and I make the children's room as comfortable and homely as soon as possible. They have spent the night with another family to make things easier for them in such a stressful time.

Basheera and I unpack the food and utensils in the kitchen and realise it's already 6.30am. We start to make tea and soon, Lynn, the vicar's wife, arrives with freshly baked scones and croissants she bought on the way. We are all so hungry and tired, so it is nice to just stand around chatting and laughing and getting to know each other. It's a pity such a travesty has brought the two religions even closer. We realise we really have so much in common and need to be able to support each other. I stand looking at all these people and realise in all my time in Stonesfield, I never really got to know them, apart from my Tuesday morning coffees I have not really got to talk to/engage with them and now see how much I have missed out on by not knowing these lovely, kind and beautiful people. God definitely can bring love and happiness out of such terrible situations.

CHAPTER ELEVEN

The world has gone into retaliation mode, hunting every possible suspect down. It seems like they are arresting hundreds of terrorists a day. There doesn't seem to be a country that isn't helping to get revenge for Max's death. Thousands of women and children are fleeing Raqqa. Much of Raqqa is in ruins, and even Moscow compared it to the Allied destruction of the German city of Dresden in World War II. They say never before has a city been so completely devastated. The entire city is just miles and miles of rubble, piles of steel pipes, windowless buildings and then you see children scavenging amongst the wreckage trying to find bits of steel and plastic they can sell to buy food. Entire families are living in bombed-out husks of buildings. It is heart-breaking. It seems like tit for tat killings are taking place. A young man walked into two mosques in New Zealand and killed 51 people. It is unfathomable that someone can just walk into places of worship and start shooting people. What makes someone think it is ok to take guns with loads of rounds of ammunition and go kill innocent people? How does your mind work when you think it is ok to kill people because of the God they serve? Why blame the religion and not just realise it's a few members gone bad? The same way a man walked into a church in Texas and killed 26 churchgoers before he was shot.

Religions all over the world can cause so much heartache yet for those who use it show God's real love can change someone's life. God encourages us to look after widows and orphans. My church in Boston lived by that scripture and when I was there many, many years ago they already had 500 adoptions from all over the world.

People from Raqqa are starting to flee everywhere. There is a mass exodus and they are walking in groups by the thousands. Germany has opened its borders to Yazidi women and children enslaved by ISIS. The only problem is that ISIS members are posing as refugees to get into Germany where they are plotting attacks there. The German government quickly start uncovering plots with the help of intelligence. They find an Algerian couple suspected of planning a terrorist attack in Berlin. They entered Germany and applied for asylum as Syrian refugees under the guise of fleeing war. It is terrible for innocent people fleeing/leaving Syria getting caught up with terrorists. Refugee camps are filling up quickly. There are camps that house up to 12,000 displaced people including a 1,000 women and children affiliated with ISIS. I read that nearly 270,000 people who have fled the Raqqa fight are still in critical need of aid and camps are overcrowded. Many people don't want to stay in the camps as they are scared they will be forgotten and many left the camps to try and enter countries illegally. Some have family members already living in different parts of Europe so they are desperate to join them. Germany has decided it won't limit the number of people it can accept. Many people in the UK are up in arms saying we need to also have an open-door policy and just accept people en masse. Parliament is trying to explain it isn't possible as we are bursting at the seams and don't have enough houses for the homeless living here and accepting these numbers of refugees can put them at risk of being homeless.

Germany realises very quickly they should have also had a limit as things start to take a turn for the worst. The refugees feel unwelcome and say their religion and culture isn't considered and they start to riot. Refugees are attacking people, raping young girls and looting businesses. The Germans are retaliating and starting to form Neo Nazi groups and are going around in groups and beating up refugees. All hell breaks loose on New Year's Eve with groups fighting in the streets, young girls getting sexually harassed and even a few rapes. The police are out in riot gear. The refugees say they know they can't get caught or go to jail as they are oppressed and it's not their fault they behave this way. People take to the streets and start marching and demanding the government steps in to protect the Germans. Women and children are living in fear.

A young girl is kidnapped at a local swimming pool. She is raped and strangled. The offender is caught and it appears he lied when he entered the country. He said he was 15 years old and his passport wasn't properly checked. It turns out he is 28 years old and you can clearly see he is a grown man and not a child. It seems the passport office didn't want to ask too many questions in case people thought they were discriminating. It seems to be going from one extreme to the next. Germany lives under a cloud. They are in fear people will bring up Hitler and they don't ever want to be tarnished with that brush. Interestingly enough there is absolutely nothing with Hitler's name on in Germany.

They refuse to remember him; well he was the biggest evil of all time and who would want to be associated with him? It's a vicious circle and hopefully can be resolved quickly as the majority of people want to live in peace and want to accept the refugees and give them a permanent home.

My church says we need to be proactive and start arranging fundraising events. We have pudding clubs, quizzes, bingo evenings and some of the fit members of the church are running marathons or cycling long distances to raise money and awareness. The usual tensions arise after these events with everyone wanting to make sure the money gets to the right people and not lining some director of a large corporation's pocket. It's as if everyone has an agenda and it's all getting out of hand. I look at the news every day and wonder if World War III will break out soon. With all the countries arming themselves with nuclear weapons soon we will be blowing each other up and the civilians will pay the price because someone with a large ego in the government thinks they need to show the world not to mess with their country.

CHAPTER TWELVE

Basheera and I meet up twice a week for a quick coffee and chat after work. The Muslim community is looking after them, taking meals around and at the same time lying very low themselves. Some idiots have tried to set the mosque alight in town. Luckily, there were a few men in the mosque praying so they were able to call the fire brigade. It could have been a lot worse, and they could have burnt to death. No arrests have been made, surprise, surprise. I do find it strange with so much CCTV around and yet the police can't seem to find the culprits. Apparently, they forgot to back up the footage and taped straight over it. The police now have someone on duty 24/7 to protect the mosque and, on Fridays, they have extra police on for protection.

The churches decide we need to join forces and do a march in the centre of the village to show our support for the Muslim community. The local MP thinks it is a brilliant idea and brings his family along to show his support. We arrange to meet at the town hall and march around the village. Lots of the Muslim community show up and we all walk together with banners, flags and boards. Children bring whistles and little drums. It is such a lovely morning walking around and talking and uniting to show our support for our brothers and sisters. There is such an amazing community spirit. People stand on the side of the road, waving and cheering us on. Some walk over and join in the march. Afterwards, we arrive back at the town hall and one of the local pizza places run by a couple of men from the mosque turn up with so many pizzas and garlic bread and we stand around talking and eating. The spirit between the two so-different religions is growing continually and to my surprise, I find out one of the older members of the mosque is married to a Christian. He told me they fell in love and never forced each other to change. They have children and have never had any problems. They married each other for love and nothing else. It proves we can just love each other with no strings attached.

It's amazing what you find out when you actually take the time to get to know one another and listen.

Once I start to really get to know Muslims, I realise how loving they are, and they do accept anyone. I meet Jews married to Muslims and Buddhists married to Muslims and they all say they were never forced to change their religion. They all eventually converted to Islam because they saw what a peaceful religion it is. Women aren't forced by the mosque to wear a hijab and a high percentage of women don't. My eyes are being opened and the prejudice is starting to fall away. In a way, Max's death has opened my eyes and made me change my views on Muslims for the good. Max's death for me was not in vain and I'm grateful that I found the good in his death. I pray many others can as well.

Slowly things are starting to go back to normal. The Imam and his family have moved back home. People in the village have moved on to the next bit of excitement in it. There is always going to be small-minded people who love to gossip and stir things but hopefully, the majority see through this and move on. It seems that ISIS has gone underground for a while, but their sleeper cells are still working and recruiting members in places like Spain and Iraq. Intelligence officials estimate there are 2,500 to 3,000 ISIS fighters still in Iraq so they won't be lying low for much longer. In the meantime, I have started to learn more about Islam and their love for Jesus, or as they call him Prophet Issa, is remarkable

As the weeks go by and I am meeting up with Abdul to discuss Islam and Christianity, I find myself slowly starting to appreciate Islam a lot more. It is so amazing to learn what a peaceful and loving religion it is. I always thought of it as a religion that dictates what you must do and what not. Now I'm learning how forgiving Allah is and how loving he is. Of course he is the same God I believe in and yes, I do believe he is merciful and forgiving.

I love how Allah asks Muslims to pray five times a day and he says just short prayers so you can connect with him. He asks that you fast once a year for a month, give 2.5% of your savings once a year to a charity of your choice and perform pilgrimage once in your lifetime to erase all the sins

It is nothing like what I thought it would be. I have now given up alcohol completely. Not that it was difficult; the two gin and tonics I drank a year won't be missed. I have stopped eating pork as well and that also isn't a problem as I was never a fan of pork. I start to buy halal meat as I find its quality better. Kosher and halal food are both good to me. My prayer life has become so much better. I make an effort to pray on my knees every morning and make sure I have a Bible study in the evenings and pray again. I also make sure I'm appropriately dressed and not praying in shorts etc. I am loving my new devotion to God. I fast the whole month of Ramadan and it is honestly one of the best things I have ever done. I enjoy having the days without food and water and reflecting on God and his faithfulness. I feel our relationship has deepened and is on a completely different level. The peace and calm I experience is wonderful and not something you can just describe to anyone. Yaz and I still make sure we go to church. Abdul and I talk for hours on how God loves obedience from us and rewards us so much with his love and blessings. It is amazing how one's mind-set can slowly change just by asking the right person questions. That is why it is absolutely important you seek answers from the right people, those with no hidden agenda and who truly grasp the teachings of Islam and the Prophet (PBUH) with tolerance and acceptance. I'm lucky God holds on to me and won't let go. He is so gracious; thank you, Lord.

****

The #UanMii is the most popular hashtag on Instagram. Young people realise how important it is to love one another as we are all God's children. They realise it needs to start with young people and to accept everyone no matter what the colour of your skin is, your religion or sexuality. As Max loved everyone and never discriminated, they want to love everyone without prejudice. A charity has been set up to support teenagers from refugee families. The Prime Minister has gotten very involved and he wants to see that the money goes to the right people who can benefit from UanMii. Celebrities have all joined in and a summer music festival has been arranged. Hyde Park is going to be the place to be seen this summer. The way everyone is getting involved, it looks like it will be more than a day event, more likely a weekend festival.

Charities are taking advantage of everyone's generosity. Homeless charities have been given permission to sell food to collect funds and increase awareness. Charities for different refugees have been given permission to sell arts and crafts from the countries they are raising money and awareness for. Churches and mosques are allowed to set up children's activities and prayer tents. Church choirs are auditioning to be backup vocals to different bands. They are trying to create one large choir from different religious organisations to sing in between band changes. It seems that all the participating artists have signed up for free so that all the money raised can go to UanMii.

I wonder if Max is looking down on us and thinking how is it possible that such a small boy could have caused such a change in people? The ripple effect is definitely taking place and it is wonderful to see it happen so quickly and with such force. People are reaching out to people they never would have approached before. The other, innocent people who have been beheaded before are included and not forgotten. They too gave their lives and we need to remember them just as we remember

Max. Their deaths must not be in vain, we need to make their families proud of them and to show we are grateful to them. Their families went through as much pain and suffering and their heartache is just as real. Some of those suffered horrific deaths at the hands of ISIS as they wanted to make a point that they were not to be messed with. Some were drowned, set alight in cages, or put in cars and bombed. They even lined them up in front of graves and got children to execute them. How will this affect these children later on in life? One day when they are old enough to be able to think about what they really did, they actually executed an innocent person. They were only guilty in the eyes of ISIS because they don't support ISIS. They even executed Muslims, so *they* weren't even exempt from death. Is this what Allah would have wanted? I think it must hurt him so much as he wants Islam to be known as a loving religion and now ISIS is a group that has gone rogue and is destroying the name of Islam.

When I arrive at our usual coffee morning, I am greeted with lots of excitement. The ladies agree need to support Max and send out an email asking who wants to join us going to the festival. We decide we need to move immediately as tickets will sell out within minutes even though it is a weekend festival with space for hundreds of thousands. Once the email goes out, we receive replies within minutes. The response is overwhelming, seems like everyone wants to go. We reach the conclusion the best thing is to get everyone to order their own tickets and we will arrange the transport. We hire a few minivans and some men offer to drive them. I go with a mixed group from the church and mosque and we travel in one of the larger minivans. The church thinks that since our Muslim brothers and sisters don't drink, no one will drink as a sign of respect. There are a few who don't agree but are quickly told, 'If you don't like the arrangement, please go ahead and get yourself to the concert but unfortunately you won't be able to sit with us.'

The day arrives and soon we picnic together and sit laughing and talking, I can see God at work. We all believe in the same God, but to us, it is through religion that we can enjoy our new friendships. My newfound knowledge of Islam has taught me so much and has made it possible for me to love and respect Muslim people even more. I love how they have taught me little things that has made my Christian life even more special. Their respect for their religion puts me to shame and has taught me that I need to do a lot more if I do want to see Jesus one day. Out of something so evil, God has turned it into something so beautiful. My new friendships are so special, and I am so grateful to God for having his hand in this difficult time and blessing all of us.

I look up and see the mixed choir singing, it is so beautiful to see women with hijabs, black women, white women, men of all colours and even children on the stage. The happiness and love radiates from the stage and the music is magical. The concert is a big success. I really hope all this effort will not be wasted and the money put to good use. I really think Max would have been so proud. I pray his parents have managed to find a little comfort from his painful death. They say the pain has been so deep and excruciating. There are days where they struggle to get out of bed and only with time has the pain started to lessen. They talked about the pain and how it never leaves you and some days it comes back with such vengeance you struggle to breathe. Being in the public eye makes it very difficult. They say grieving has been difficult at times as there is always meetings or something they need to attend. They feel as if they are on tenterhooks, scared someone will mention Max and they will fall apart. Then again other people are also on tenterhooks with them as they don't want to say the wrong thing. My heart breaks for them as they stand on the stage. They announce that this concert has given them something to focus on and knowing that Max would have loved it so much, sharing that whenever they were making a decision about the concert, they always asked themselves what would Max have wanted?

Parents start to live through their children and to have them ripped away from you so painfully is heart-wrenching. To me they are remarkable, the courage and strength they have shown is on a different level. I have seen strength in these people that I never knew was possible. They have, through their pain, shown others that it is important to love one another no matter what. So, in honour of Max, ice cream sundae building stalls have been set up around the venue. They want other children to get as much pleasure of building the perfect sundae as Max used to get. Looking around I can see they are a success as there are children all over with bowls of ice cream laden with sweets. No one will be sleeping tonight with all those E numbers.

As they continue talking about Max, I feel a tear run down my face and thank God again for protecting Yasmin. She is my joy in life and one of my greatest achievements. Her cheekiness, love for life and her caring nature is all I can ask for. I even love it when she continuously calls out *mum, mum, mum* until I acknowledge her. God is good.

As I'm sitting in the sun enjoying God's abundance of blessings suddenly Abdul falls down next to me, 'So my love, when am I seeing you in hijab?' 'Soon Abdul, Inshallah.'

To my daughters, love you both to the moon and back.

Thank you Reem Darwish for your patience and proofreading my COVID project over and over again.

Thank you Supun Sukitha for my beautiful book cover.

Printed in Great Britain
by Amazon